LITTLE SIMON
An imprint of Simon & Schuster Children's Publishing Division
1230 Avenue of the Americas, New York, New York 10020
First Little Simon paperback edition October 2017. Copyright © 2017 by Simon & Schuster, Inc. All rights reserved, including the right of reproduction in whole or in part in any form. LITTLE SIMON is a registered trademark of Simon & Schuster, Inc., and associated colophon is a trademark of Simon & Schuster, Inc. For information about special discounts for bulk purchases, please contact Simon & Schuster Special Sales at 1-866-506-1949 or business@simonandschuster.com. The Simon & Schuster Speakers Bureau can bring authors to your live event. For more information or to book an event contact the Simon & Schuster Speakers Bureau at 1-866-248-3049 or visit our website at www.simonspeakers.com. Series designed by Laura Roode. Book designed by Hannah Frece. The text of this book was set in Usherwood.
Manufactured in the United States of America 0917 MTN 10 9 8 7 6 5 4 3 2 1
Cataloging-in-Publication Data is available from the Library of Congress.
ISBN 978-1-4814-9986-6 (hc)
ISBN 978-1-4814-9985-9 (pbk)
ISBN 978-1-4814-9987-3 (eBook)

the adventures of

SOPHIE MOUSE

12

Journey to the Crystal Cave

By Poppy Green • Illustrated by Jennifer A. Bell

LITTLE SIMON

New York London Toronto Sydney New Delhi

Contents

~ Chapter 1 ~

Hide-and-seek

"Ready or not, here I come!" Sophie shouted.

She opened her eyes and looked around. Owen and Hattie were gone. The three friends were playing hide-and-seek by Owen's house. Sophie was the seeker.

She listened for a rustle of leaves or a snap of a twig. She sniffed the air. Really, though, she didn't need any clues. There were only two good hiding places in Owen's yard.

First, Sophie checked inside the hollow log. It was a tight squeeze for Hattie or herself, but Owen fit easily.

Sophie peered inside. "Found you!" she cried.

Owen wriggled out. "Aww," he

moaned. "That was quick."

Next Sophie scurried over to a baby fir tree. Hattie was pretty well camouflaged by the needles. But Sophie could see her shoes.

"Hi, Hattie," Sophie said casually.

Hattie sighed and climbed out of the tree. "We need a new place to play this game," she said.

"Yes," Sophie agreed. "Somewhere we don't know as well. With different places to hide!"

"Like where?" Owen asked.

The three of them were quiet as they thought it over.

A picture popped into Sophie's mind. Lots of large evergreen trees grew along a brook. The lower branches arched down to the ground, creating sheltered areas underneath.

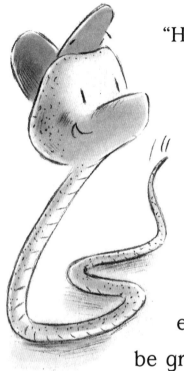

"How about Butterfly Brook?" Sophie suggested.

"Oh yeah!" Owen cried.

Hattie agreed. "All those little hideaways!" she exclaimed. "They'll be great for hiding!"

Owen ran inside to tell his mom where they were going. Then they set off together for Butterfly Brook.

They took their time getting there, stopping off at fun places along the

way. They played on the rope swing at the playground by Sophie's house. They took a few rides down Birch Tree Slide.

By the time they arrived at the brook, Sophie was eager to start a new round of hide-and-seek. "Who wants to be 'it'?" she asked.

"I got found first last time," Owen said, sounding a little mopey. "So I guess it's me this time."

"Okay," Hattie agreed. "How far can we go to hide? What are the boundaries?"

Hattie liked to have all the rules spelled out clearly.

Sophie shrugged. "Don't go out of earshot?" she suggested. "That way, if Owen can't find us, he can call us to come out."

Owen nodded. He sat down on a piece of driftwood. "Okay!" he said, closing his eyes. "I'm starting to count! One, two, three . . ."

Hattie raced off toward the trees. Sophie scampered upstream, filled with a sense of adventure.

She was determined to find the best hiding spot ever!

— Chapter 2 —

A Light in the Dark

Sophie came to an area where several large rocks rose from the water. She hopped from one to the next to cross the brook.

Then Sophie dashed into the trees.

Her eyes darted around frantically, looking for a good hiding spot.

She noticed a cluster of large mushrooms. Sophie managed to squeeze herself underneath one of them. She sat there, motionless, for a few minutes.

This is good, she told herself. *I think. Though maybe I should have gone a little farther. Nah. I bet Owen won't cross the brook right away.*

She was quiet and still for another minute.

I wonder if he can see my feet from far away, she thought.

The minutes passed. Sophie got more and more restless.

I need a better spot! she decided suddenly.

She crawled out from under the mushroom and scurried off.

Sophie stopped for a moment by a tangle of tree roots. *Not enough cover,* she decided—and kept on going.

She came to a dense thicket of
brambleberry.

Ow! she thought, trying to crawl
in. *Too prickly.* There was no way
she was hiding in there.

So Sophie kept looking, changing direction a few times.

At last, she saw a large rock formation. *Hmm,* she thought, hurrying
closer. She walked around one side,
only to find an opening.

Sophie peered inside. It was a
cave! Or maybe a tunnel?

Perfect! Sophie decided as she

stepped inside. *It's so dark. Even if Owen looks in here, he won't be able to see me.*

A few steps in, Sophie could barely see where she was going. She used her hands to feel her way along the

craggy wall. She stretched one foot forward carefully before taking each step.

Just a few more, Sophie told herself. *Owen will never come this far in.*

Then, strangely, the way ahead started to get . . . lighter. And . . . brighter.

At first Sophie thought she was imagining it.

But no. There was a purple glow coming from inside the cave. Now Sophie could make out the outlines of the rocks. Up ahead, the path curved to the left. The source of the

glowing light was somewhere around the bend.

The light grew brighter with each step, until—

"So-phie . . ."

Her name echoed faintly off the cave walls. Sophie turned around. It sounded like Owen and Hattie, calling out *together.* But they sounded so far away.

Sophie was torn. She wanted to see where the light was coming from. But she also didn't want her friends to worry.

She knew she had to go.

Sophie backtracked to the cave entrance. Out in the sunlight, she blinked as her eyes adjusted. Hattie and Owen were nowhere to be seen.

Sophie called out as loudly as she could. "Owen? Hattie? Where are you?"

Chapter 3

Now You See It, Now You Don't

Sophie walked and walked, following the sound of Hattie's and Owen's voices. Their calls were louder now. They sounded closer. Sophie kept expecting to find her friends around the next tree.

"I'm here!" she called. "Hello?"

"We're over here! Walk this way!" came Owen's voice.

Which way?

It felt to Sophie as if they were all walking in circles around one another. Finally, Sophie poked her head around a stump and there they were!

"Sophie!" Owen cried. "We've been looking all over for you!"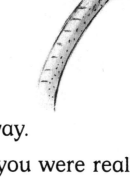

"You definitely win," Hattie told Sophie. "Owen found me almost right away. Wherever *you* were, you were really hidden!"

Sophie smiled mischievously. "I was," she said. "I'll show you."

Usually, Sophie would keep a winning hiding place a secret. That way, she could use it again the next time

they came to play. But the cave was too special. She *had* to show it to her friends.

Maybe we can find out where that glow is coming from, Sophie thought.

Sophie turned and led them

through the woods. Then she stopped
and looked around. "I *thought* this
was the way," she said. "But . . . now
I'm not sure."

She walked on slowly. Did this
look familiar? In her quest to find
Hattie and Owen, she had been using

her ears to follow their voices. She hadn't paid attention to landmarks.

Sophie saw a wall of rocks up ahead. "Oh! Here it is!" she cried.

She rushed over. But there was no cave opening.

"Huh," said Sophie. "That's funny. I could have sworn this was it."

"What?" Owen asked.

"The cave!" Sophie replied. "The cave where I hid." She walked the full length of the rock wall. "But it's definitely not *here*."

Hattie shrugged. "Maybe this isn't the right rock wall," she said. "There are a lot of them around, especially closer to the brook."

They walked on and kept looking.

Along the way, they found a few more rocky groupings.

But no cave.

Sophie sighed. "I have no idea where it is," she admitted.

Eventually, they heard rushing

water. They followed it and came out of the woods on the bank of the brook.

By now, the sun was sinking lower in the sky. The autumn days were getting shorter. Sophie knew she should head home for dinner.

"Oh, I *wish* we'd found it," she moaned on the walk home. "It wasn't just the cave I wanted to show you. There was something inside—something glowing!"

"Glowing?" Hattie said doubtfully.

"Really!" Sophie cried. "Not like a firefly kind of glow. It was different— like a purple light." Sophie sighed heavily. "But I didn't get a chance to see what was making it. Maybe I never will."

Chapter 4

Mrs. Mouse's Good Advice

Sophie got home just before her mother. Mrs. Mouse had worked a long, busy Saturday at her bakery in Pine Needle Grove.

Mr. Mouse had dinner ready—a thick potato-parsnip-pumpkin stew. Sophie's little brother, Winston, had set the table.

Soon they were sitting down to

dinner. They took turns sharing the events of their day. "Did you have fun with Owen and Hattie?" Mr. Mouse asked when it was Sophie's turn to share.

Sophie nodded. "We played hide-and-seek at Butterfly Brook."

Before she could mention the cave, Winston interrupted. "Aw! How come I couldn't go too?"

Mr. Mouse reminded Winston he got to go apple picking with James Rabbit and his family. But Winston was still jealous. He always complained that Sophie's adventures were more exciting than his.

After dinner, Winston cleared the table and Sophie washed dishes. Then she went up to her room. She propped up a blank canvas on her easel.

She wanted to paint what she remembered of the cave.

She mixed up a special shade of gray for the rock walls. For the shadows, she pulled out a black paint she made from black-eyed Susan seeds. *And I'll need hyacinth purple for the mysterious glowing light,* Sophie decided.

Ready to paint, Sophie opened her box of brushes. It was empty.

Sophie remembered: She'd brought them to an art workshop at the library the other day. She'd packed them in her travel pouch.

But where was the travel pouch?

Sophie looked all over her room— on her desk, shelves, and nightstand.

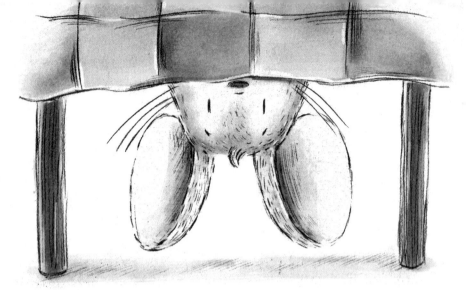

She checked under her bed, inside her satchel, and on top of her dresser. No luck.

Sophie heard her mom's voice in her head. *Go to the last place you remember having it. Then retrace your steps.* That's what she always said when Sophie or Winston couldn't find something.

So Sophie went down to the front door. She knew she'd had the pouch on her walk home from the library. She remembered putting it down somewhere to take off her shoes. Sophie looked around the entryway.

The pouch was nowhere to be seen.

Sophie remembered she'd been hungry. She'd gone to the kitchen for a snack.

Sophie checked the kitchen counter. No pouch.

She had taken a snack plate down from the dish cabinet. So she checked the cabinet. The pouch wasn't there, either.

Then Sophie had opened the bread box to look for muffins.

Now she peeked inside again.

"Aha!" she cried.

The pouch was there, behind the scones.

Sophie smiled. Her mom's trick *was* a good trick! It almost always worked for finding things.

Halfway back up the stairs, Sophie stopped in her tracks.

Could it work for finding the cave?

— Chapter 5 —

Search Party

The next morning, Sophie invited Winston to go with her to Butterfly Brook. She'd told him about the cave and her mission for today.

"If I start from where we began the game," Sophie said, "maybe I can retrace my steps *to* the cave!"

Winston trotted along at Sophie's side. "I've never been in a real cave

before!" he said excitedly.

Sophie hadn't *exactly* told Winston what it was like inside. She thought it might scare him off. And she kind of wanted some company.

I'll warn him before we go in, she decided. *If we even find it!*

At Butterfly Brook, Sophie marched straight over to the driftwood Owen had sat on.

"Here's where Owen was count-
ing," she told Winston. "From here,
I went upstream and crossed the
brook."

She led the way, showing Winston
a good route to take across the rocks.

On the other side, they went into the trees.

Sophie pointed at the cluster of mushrooms. "I hid there at first," she said.

She passed the tangle of tree roots and the brambleberry thicket.

Then, with Winston right behind her, Sophie came over a rise.

There!

Up ahead was the large rock

formation. She knew right away.
This was it.

Sophie picked up her pace.

"Wait for me!" Winston cried, trying to keep up.

But Sophie reached the rocks first.
She walked around the side and . . .

"Look, Winston!" she cried.

Winston caught up. He stood at Sophie's side, peering into the cave.

"You found it!" Winston exclaimed. Then he kept right on going, straight into the darkness. "What's inside?"

"Winston! Slow down!" Sophie

called after him. "It's hard to see in there!"

Sophie went in after him, trying to catch up. She looked down to find solid footing. When she looked up again, Sophie could barely make out Winston's shadowy form up ahead.

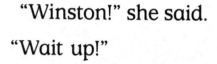

"Winston!" she said. "Wait up!"

Just then a high-pitched noise filled the cave.

Sophie froze as it echoed off the rock walls.

She heard Winston whimper. "What was that?" he whispered.

"I don't know," Sophie whispered back. "But I think we better not go any farther—"

Squeak! Squeak! Screeeeeech!

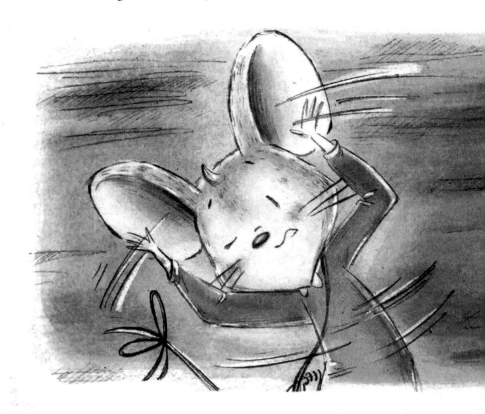

That time, the sound seemed to come from right behind her. Sophie spun around.

Squeak! Now it was by her ear. Sophie swatted at it, and then she tripped over a rock and fell.

Squeak! Squeak! Screeeeeech!

Winston tripped over Sophie and landed next to her.

It seemed like the noise was all around them—all at once!

Sophie got to her feet, then helped Winston up. Holding hands, they stumbled along the rocky path.

Sunlight from the cave entrance lit the way forward until—finally!—they were outside.

Sophie stood catching her breath, staring back into the cave.

Winston looked at Sophie, his eyes wide with fright.

"Sophie," he said, "what was *that*?"

Chapter 6

Believe It or Not

When is recess? Sophie wondered, watching the schoolhouse clock.

It had been a busy Monday morning at Silverlake Elementary. Mrs. Wise had gone over the answers from Friday's math quiz. She had led them through a science lab on different types of rocks. Then she'd handed out a new list of spelling words. Writing in their notebooks, students had to use each word in a sentence.

All of Sophie's sentences had something in common.

Sophie was itching to talk to her

Sophie

Into: We walked slowly into the cave.
Because: We ran out because of the scary noises all around.
Again: Winston said he would never go in there again.

friends! There
had been
no time to
tell them her
news before
school started.

When Mrs. Wise
rang the bell for recess, Sophie prac-
tically jumped out of her seat.

Outside, Sophie ran over to Hattie
and Owen. They were starting a game
of hopscotch with Ben and Ellie.

"We found it!" she told them.
"The cave! Winston and I found it
yesterday!"

"You did?" Owen replied.

"What was making that glowing light?" Hattie asked eagerly.

Sophie's whiskers drooped. "I don't know," she said. "We ran out of there as soon as we heard the shrieking."

Hattie and Owen stared at Sophie.

Ben and Ellie, who were looking for good hopscotch rocks, turned to look at her too.

"Shrieking?" cried Hattie in alarm.

Sophie reconsidered. "Okay, maybe not *shrieking,* exactly," she said. She described the high-pitched sound that had scared them out of the cave.

"It was so startling!" she said. "Especially because we couldn't see anything. So now there are two mysteries to solve in that cave!"

Ellie threw her rock into the first square and started hopping. "Glowing and shrieking?" she said. "Are you sure you weren't imagining that?

The mind can play tricks, you know. Especially when you're scared. And caves *are* spooky!"

"And echoey," Ben added. "Little noises sound bigger in caves."

Sophie frowned. Didn't her friends believe her?

"Well, I know what I saw and heard," she insisted. "And I'm going to find out what's in there." She looked at Hattie and Owen. "You'll come with me, right?"

They didn't answer right away.
Owen looked at Hattie. Hattie
shrugged.

"Isn't it more fun if it just *stays*
a mystery?" Hattie tried.

Sophie put her hands on her hips
and shook her head no.

Owen sighed. "All right. We'll
come."

"But," said Hattie, putting up a hand, "this time, we're going prepared."

They agreed they'd have to wait for Saturday to return to the cave.

"Can you make a map to show the way to the cave?" Hattie asked

Sophie. "We don't want to waste time walking in circles."

Sophie nodded. "I can do that."

"Owen, you and I can bring supplies. We need lanterns and rope," Hattie said.

"On it!" Owen replied.

Of course! Sophie thought. *Why*

didn't I think of that? Then she smiled. Hattie was so practical.

They were going to be *very* well-prepared cave explorers!

which way?

The three friends stood at the cave entrance. They had found it easily this time.

Hattie and Owen had the lanterns they had brought from home. Owen handed one to Sophie.

Hattie took out a box of matches. She was a Forest Scout and had gotten her fire safety badge. So she

was the one to carefully light each lantern's candle.

Sophie looked at her friends. "Ready?" she asked. "Let's go!" And she led the way into the cave.

The three lanterns made lots of light. Unlike last time, Sophie could

clearly see the way ahead. It was a rock-walled tunnel, curving gradually to the left.

She looked up at the cave ceiling. At the entrance, it was almost low enough to touch. But farther in, it got higher and higher.

Suddenly, Sophie detected some-thing moving at her side. She jumped—then laughed. She'd been spooked by their long shadows, cast onto the cave wall by the candlelight.

The friends covered ground quickly. Before long, Sophie was sure they had come farther than she had on her own or with Winston.

The cave was quiet. No shrieking. No mysterious noises. The only
sounds were their footsteps echoing
off the walls.

And where was
the glowing light?
Was their lantern
light drowning
it out?

*Or did I just
imagine it after all?*

Sophie stopped at a
fork in the path. Hattie and
Owen came up and stood on either
side.

"Now what?" Sophie said. "Right or left?"

Hattie held her lantern high, trying to see down each tunnel. It was no help. Both paths looked the same.

"I guess we just pick one," Hattie suggested.

Sophie's eyes fell on the coil of rope tied to Hattie's backpack. She had an idea!

"Or we could split up," Sophie said.

Hattie shook her head. "No way. I vote we stay together."

Sophie took the rope. "Wait, listen.

Maybe we can use our rope to keep us connected."

She held one end and tied the other end around Owen's waist.

"Two of us go one way, and one goes the other," said Sophie. "We'll go just until the rope pulls tight and we can't go any farther. Then we'll follow the rope back and talk about what we found."

Owen nodded. "That way, we won't lose one another."

Hattie frowned. "But who is going to go alone?"

Owen looked down at the rope around his waist. "Well, I'm already tied on," he said. "I'll go by myself. See you back here in a minute."

He slithered away down the right-hand tunnel.

— Chapter · 8 —

A Missing Explorer

The left-hand tunnel sloped slightly downward. Sophie could feel the air growing cooler. "I think we're headed underground," she said to Hattie.

They hopped over a puddle formed by a slow drip-drip of water from the ceiling. They scrambled over a large boulder partially blocking the way.

Up ahead, the tunnel turned

sharply to the right. They had almost reached the turn when Sophie abruptly stopped.

The rope was taut. She couldn't go any farther without letting go.

Sophie and Hattie turned around and went back, coiling up the rope as they walked. When they got to the fork, Owen wasn't there.

"Owen!" Sophie called down the right-hand tunnel. "Come back, okay?"

There was no answer.

"Owen?" Hattie called.

They held up their lanterns and followed the rope down the right-hand tunnel. "Owen, where are you?" Sophie called again. *Why isn't he answering?* she wondered.

They followed the rope over a pile of pebbles and around another bend.

Hattie stopped and pointed up ahead.

Sophie saw it too. The other end of the rope lay there on the ground. She and Hattie cast their lantern light all around.

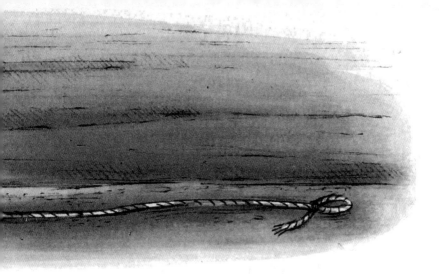

But Owen was nowhere to be seen.

Sophie and Hattie stared at each other in shock.

"Owen!" Sophie shouted frantically. "Owen!"

Squeak! Squeak! Screeeeeech!

In a flash of noise and flapping wings, Sophie felt something swoop past the tip of her nose.

"Ahh!" Sophie cried. She flinched and took a step backward.

A second later, the creature was flapping around Hattie's head. Hattie ducked and cried out. "Sophie! What is it?"

Squeak! Squeak! Screeeeeech!

Sophie raised her lantern, trying to get a good look. Whatever it was, was moving fast—darting this way and that!

"I don't know!" Sophie called. "Hattie, come toward me!"

They linked arms and backed away from the creature. Again and again, it swooped down from the cave ceiling. Each time, Sophie and Hattie took another step backward, until—

"Aaaaaaaaah!" Sophie and Hattie cried out together.

The ground fell away beneath their feet. They were tumbling backward, and then—*oof!*—they hit the ground and they were sliding! They slid down, down, down on a smooth, slippery ramp, almost like a slide.

Then, gradually, the slide leveled off and the girls rolled to a stop. Sophie rubbed her eyes and looked around.

Owen was standing over them, bathed in purple light.

"Owen!" Hattie cried.

Owen helped them up. "Are you guys okay?" he asked, concerned.

Sophie dusted herself off. "I think so," she replied. "What—what happened? We were looking for you and then . . ."

Her words trailed off as her eyes
moved from Owen's face to the
magical sight behind him.

Sophie gasped.

They were standing in a huge
cavern filled with glittering blue,
pink, and purple crystals. Together,
they cast a beautiful purplish light.

Large crystal columns poked up from the ground, reaching halfway to the ceiling.

Other crystals hung down from the ceiling like fancy light fixtures.

They clung to the walls, sparkling and shiny. And they all seemed to be glowing.

"Where—where are we?" Sophie said, filled with awe.

Owen shook his head. "I don't know," he said.

The three friends stood in silence, taking in the beauty of the cave.

From somewhere close behind them came a tiny, squeaky voice.

"You're in Crystal Cave!"

~ Chapter 9 ~

Don't Mind My Manners

Sophie, Hattie, and Owen whirled around. A small, furry brown bat was hanging upside down from a nearby crystal.

"Ahhhhhh!" Sophie shouted.

"Eeeeeeeep!" the bat squeaked, startled by Sophie's shout.

It was a very familiar sound—high-pitched, almost a shriek!

Sophie covered her ears until the bat quieted down and the echoes faded. Then she eyed him suspiciously.

"Wait a minute," said Sophie. She put her hands on her hips. "Were you the one attacking us up there?" She pointed up the slide.

The bat nodded. Then he shook

his head. "No," he squeaked. "I mean, yes. I mean . . . I wasn't trying to attack you."

Hattie and Sophie looked at each other in disbelief. "It kind of felt that way," Hattie said gently.

The bat covered his face with a wing. He peeked sheepishly out at them. "I was trying to help you find your friend," he said. "I saw him slip

down the slide. Then I saw you come looking for him."

Sophie was confused. "You were trying to make us fall down too? So we'd find him?"

The bat nodded.

"Maybe you could have told us instead?" Hattie pointed out.

The bat hid behind his wing again. "Sorry," he squeaked. "I . . . don't get a lot of visitors in here. I guess I don't have the best manners."

Sophie's heart melted. "No, *we're* sorry," she said. "This is your cave. We didn't mean to barge in. I was just so curious about what was in here."

She introduced herself, and Hattie and Owen too.

"Pleased to meet you," the bat replied. "My name's Jet."

Sophie looked up and around at the crystals. "Your home is so beautiful, Jet."

"How do the crystals glow like that?" Owen asked.

Jet flapped his wings and flew in a circle around one crystal. He explained that they were made of a mineral called fluorite.

"Way up at the top of the cavern," Jet said, "there's a skylight—an opening in the ceiling. For a short time each day, when the sun is high, light streams in. It hits the crystals, which makes them glow in the dark for hours afterward." Jet came in for a landing next to Sophie. "My grandpa says it's called *photoluminescence*."

"Your grandpa?" Owen said. "Does he live here too?"

Jet nodded. "My whole family lives here," he said. "See!"

He pointed to an area high up on the cavern wall. Dozens and dozens

of bats hung upside down from crystal ledges.

"Wow!" said Hattie. "You have a big family!"

"Yep," the bat replied. "Brothers, sisters, my mom and dad, aunts, uncles, cousins, and grandparents. They're all here!"

A couple of the bats waved hello. But most hung there motionless. Their wings were wrapped tightly around their bodies as if they were in sleeping bags. They peeked out at the visitors with curiosity.

"They're not used to company either," Jet explained. "It's kind of

why we live in here. It's peaceful. And quiet." Then he laughed. "Well, *usually* it is," he added.

Sophie nodded. Then it hit her. The bat family would probably prefer to be left alone.

"Well, we should get going," said Sophie. "We all have homework to do, anyway."

Owen was staring dreamily into a crystal. "We do?" he said.

But Hattie understood. "Yep, we do," she said, nudging Owen toward the exit. "Jet, could you help us find the way out?"

Chapter 10

The *Secret* Crystal Cave

On Monday morning at school, all the students were hanging up their coats. Ellie hung hers on the coat hook next to Sophie's.

"So did you go back to that cave?" Ellie asked Sophie.

Ben looked over, interested to hear the answer.

Hattie and Owen glanced over

too. What would Sophie say?

"Yes, we did!" Sophie replied. "And you know what? That spooky noise? It *wasn't* just my imagination."

"It wasn't?" Ellie said, intrigued.

Sophie had *so* wanted to take a crystal home. She had almost asked Jet if she could. That way, they could show Ellie and Ben and everyone at school. Proof of the Crystal Cave!

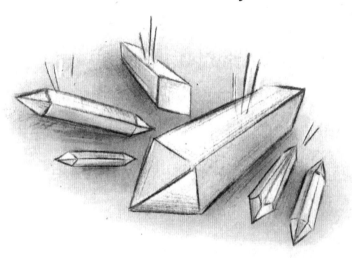

But then Sophie had realized what would happen next. Everyone *else* would want to go to see the cave for themselves.

How would the bat family ever get any peace?

So in the end, Sophie hadn't asked for a crystal. Instead, she had asked Hattie and Owen if they could keep a secret—for the bat family.

"Nope! It wasn't my imagination," Sophie repeated. She shrugged. "It was just a bat. A really nice bat."

She looked at Hattie and Owen and winked.

The secret of Crystal Cave was safe with them.

The End

Meet the CRITTER club

Four best friends.
Lots of animals saved.
Tons of fun along the way.

DaiSY DREAMER

Imagine more books, activities, and adventures at
inthemiddlebooks.com.

And tell them Daisy sent you!

the adventures of

SOPHIE MOUSE

For excerpts, activities, and more about
these adorable tales & tails, visit
AdventuresofSophieMouse.com!

31901060751627